GIRLS CAN BE ANYTHING

by NORMA KLEIN

illustrated by ROY DOTY

Anytime
BOOKS

E. P. Dutton & Co., Inc. New York

This Anytime Book edition first published in 1975
by E. P. Dutton & Co., Inc., New York

Text copyright © 1973 by Norma Klein
Illustrations copyright © 1973 by Roy Doty

Published simultaneously in Canada by Clarke,
Irwin & Company Limited, Toronto and Vancouver

ISBN: 0-525-45029-7   LCC: 72-85258

Printed in the U.S.A.
First printing, April 1975

To JENNY
(who, when she grows up,
would like to be a painter,
join the circus,
and work at Baskin-Robbins,
making ice cream cones)

"Now we will play Hospital," said Adam Sobel. "I will be the doctor and you will be the nurse."

Adam Sobel was Marina's best friend in her kindergarten class. They went home on the bus together and at school, in the yard, they sat and pretended to fish. They were the only ones in the class who could do the lion puzzle and get all the pieces of the mane together. Usually Marina liked the games Adam thought up, but this time she said, "I want to be the doctor too."

"You can't be doctor if *I'm* doctor," Adam said.

"Why not?" said Marina.

"There can't be two doctors," Adam said.

"So, *you* be the nurse and *I'll* be the doctor," Marina said.

"That's not the way it goes," Adam said. He was already putting on the white doctor costume that was in the costume box. "Girls are always nurses and boys are always doctors."

"Why is that?" said Marina.

"That's just the way it is," Adam said. "Could I have the stethoscope, please, Nurse?"

That night Marina told her father at dinner, "I don't like Adam Sobel at all."

"Oh?" Father said. "I thought he used to be your favorite."

"He used to be," Marina said, "but you know what he said today?"

"What?" asked Father.

"He said girls can't be doctors. They have to just be nurses."

"Well, that's just plain silly!" her father said. "Of *course* they can be doctors."

"They can?" asked Marina.

"Certainly they can," Father replied. "Why, your Aunt Rosa is a doctor. You know that."

"But is she a real one?" Marina said.

"She sure is, as real as they come," Father said.

"Does she work in a hospital and wear a white uniform?" Marina wanted to know.

"She does," Father said. "In fact, she works in the very hospital where you were born. You know what she does there?"

"What?" said Marina.

"She's a surgeon," Father said. "That's hard work, you know."

The next day at school, Marina said to Adam, "I have an aunt who's a doctor. She's a surgeon."

"Is she a real doctor?" Adam wanted to know.

"Of *course* she's real," Marina said. "She comes to our house for dinner. She even has a white uniform. . . . Lots of women are doctors. I might be one. I might be one that takes care of animals."

"That kind is called a veterinarian," Adam said. He knew a lot of long words.

"I could have my own hospital and dogs and cats would come to see me and I would make them better," Marina said. "That's the kind of doctor *I* want to be."

"I don't even want to *be* a doctor," Adam said.

"What do you want to be?" asked Marina.

"I think I want to be a pilot," Adam said.

"You mean, you'd have your own airplane and fly it from place to place?"

"Yes," Adam said. "Why don't we play airplane right now?"

"Okay," said Marina. "How do we do it?"

"Well," said Adam, "this is the plane and I sit in front driving."

"What do *I* do?" said Marina.

"You're the stewardess," Adam said. "You walk around in back and give people drinks."

So Marina poured some water in paper cups left over from juice and crackers time and walked around and gave them to all the imaginary passengers. She always asked them first if they wanted tea, coffee, or juice.

Finally, she went over to where Adam was and asked,
"What are you doing?"

"I'm still driving the plane," Adam said. "Oh oh—
here we come. . . . It might be a crash landing. . . .
Better look out."

"You know what?" Marina said.

"What?" said Adam, who was keeping his eyes on the place where the plane had to land.

"I think *I* want to be a pilot," Marina said.

"*You* can't be a pilot," Adam said.

"If I want to, I can," Marina said.

"Girls can't be pilots," Adam said. "They have to be stewardesses."

"But that's dull," said Marina. And she went off and began to drive her own pretended plane.

That night in bed Marina said to her mother, "Adam Sobel is so *bad*."

"Is he?" her mother said. "What did he do?"

"He said girls can't drive planes," Marina said. "He said they have to be stewardesses."

"That's not true," Mother said.

"Then, how come he said it?" Marina asked.

"Maybe he didn't know," Mother answered. "There was a picture of a woman in the newspaper just the other day, and she's been flying her own plane for fifteen years."

"Does she fly with people in it?" Marina asked.

"Of course!" said Mother.

"Does she fly it all by herself?" Marina said.

"Well, she has a co-pilot," Mother said. "Pilots always have co-pilots to help them."

"Mommy?"

"Yes, darling."

"If I was a pilot, would you and Daddy fly with me in my plane?"

"We certainly would."

"Would I be a good pilot, do you think?" Marina asked.

"I think you would," Mother said.

The next day at school Marina told Adam, "Today you can be my co-pilot. I'm going to be a pilot like that lady in the paper who has her own plane."

"What lady is that?" Adam said.

"Oh, I guess you didn't see her picture," Marina said. "Her plane has people in it and everything. Even her mother and father fly in it with her."

"Who is the stewardess in that plane?" Adam said.

"It's a self-service plane," Marina said. "In the back there's a little machine and you get your drinks by putting in a nickel."

"That sounds like a good idea," Adam said. He let Marina be pilot and he was co-pilot and read the map and told her where to go. There was almost a crash landing, but Marina landed in a grassy field and everyone got out safely.

That afternoon Mrs. Darling read them a story about a king and queen. They wore long red robes and had yellow crowns on their heads.

On the way home in the bus Marina said, "How about being a king? Or a queen?"

Adam thought about that for a minute. "No."

"You could have a red robe," Marina said. "You could have a crown."

Adam shook his head. "That wouldn't be comfortable. Anyway, kings and queens don't *do* anything anymore. It would be dull."

"Maybe that's true," Marina said.

"What I'd like to be," Adam said, "is president. That's *better* than being a king."

"President of what?" Marina wanted to know.

"Just president."

"You mean *The* President?" Marina said.

"That's right," Adam said.

"What would you do if you were president?" Marina asked.

"Oh," answered Adam, "I would sit in a big room with a rug on the floor and a big desk and I would sign papers and everyone would have to do whatever I said."

"Maybe tomorrow we can play President," Marina said.

"Okay," Adam said.

"Only, the thing is," Marina said, "what would *I* be while you were president?"

"You could be my wife."

"What would I do if I were your wife?" asked Marina.

"Well, you could cook dinner and get the newspaper ready when I got home," Adam said. "Sometimes you could ride in a car with me and we could wave at people and they would throw confetti at us."

"That sounds like fun," Marina said, "only, Adam?"

"Listen," Adam said. "One thing I *know*. There's *never* been a woman president."

That night after supper Marina said to her mother and father, "I don't know what we're going to *do* with Adam Sobel. He says such silly things."

"What did he say today that was so silly?" her father said.

"He said there never was a woman president," Marina said.

There was a pause.

"Isn't he a silly boy!" Marina said. "I call him a dum-dum."

"Well, it's true, there's never been a woman President of the United States," Mother said.

"Have there been women presidents of other places?" said Marina.

"Other countries have had important women leaders," Father said. "Mrs. Gandhi in India. Mrs. Meir in Israel."

GOLDA MEIR   INDIRA GANDHI

The next morning Marina said to Adam, "Adam, you know, *you* can be a pilot or a doctor. You know what I'm going to be?"

"What?" Adam said.

"I'm going to be the first woman President! . . . You can be my husband."

"What would I do?" Adam said.

"You would fly our plane and fly me from place to place so I could give speeches," Marina said.

"It seems like according to you girls can be anything they want," Adam said.

"Well, that's just the way it is now," Marina said. "Will you fly me to where I can give my talk?"

"Okay, but after you give your talk, you have to fly me back so I can give *my* talk," Adam said.

"Okay," Marina said.

So Adam flew the plane to where Marina had to give her talk, and she gave it.

Then Marina flew Adam to where he had to give his talk, and he gave it.

Then there was a big Presidential dinner with potato chips, Coca-Cola, lollipops, Marshmallows, Juicy Fruit gum, and Tootsie Rolls for dessert.

Both Presidents thought it was delicious.

Paperbacks You'll Enjoy Anytime